THE KING

Hecate's Rebellion Book 3

Jade Hayes

TCA Publishing LLC

CHAPTER 1

"M aster."

Hades looked up from the missive that just crossed his desk to see one of his house servants standing in the doorway to his office, eyes downcast. He clutched his hands together in front, the sinewy muscles twitching beneath his black as night flesh.

"Yes, Peilas?"

The demon looked up, his red eyes flitting to his own briefly. "They have arrived, sire."

An evil smile spread over Hades's face. Peilas bowed, backing quickly from the room and darting away.

It was about time. He had been waiting for this for the last eighty-nine days.

He slid his chair back and stood, grabbing his staff from where it leaned against the bookcase behind him. The light that filled the intricate scrollwork swirled angrily at his touch. Distaste soured his mouth as he thought of having to give up the soul it contained. Not only did it go against the grain to release a soul from the underworld, but this particular soul was one of the most unique and intriguing he ever had the pleasure of holding.

As if it could sense his hesitancy to return it to its owner, the soul pulsed again within the staff.

"Yeah, yeah," he muttered, striding towards the door. "I know. I promised."

Making his way down the long corridor toward the front of his house—castle, really—his thoughts turned to what was coming his way. If those four humans had actually captured Hecate alive, it would be worth relinquishing his hold on Leo's soul. He was looking forward to making the goddess pay for her attempted mutiny.

As he reached the foyer, the large black-lacquered doors swung open to reveal the humans he sent to retrieve Hecate.

His eyes roamed over the quartet, noting the fatigue and sorrow etched on their faces, before his gaze caught on Leo Devereaux, the owner of the soul currently contained in his staff. The man looked pissed. He sensed Leo wanted to pummel him to a pulp, but wisely kept the urge in check. Hades couldn't really fault him. He would want to murder him, too, if he had taken his soul.

Mentally, he shrugged. He knew he was an asshole and didn't care. Came with being the god of the dead.

Planting his feet, he stood just inside the door, trying to keep his own expression blank as he noted the prone goddess floating next to Leo. He could hear her heart beating. They *had* taken her alive.

"Welcome," Hades intoned. "You made it with just under a day to spare."

Leo sucked in a deep breath and stepped forward, unconscious goddess in tow. "We did, and we brought what you asked. Now it's time for you to hold up your end of the deal."

Hades hummed softly and stepped forward until he was only a few feet away. He tilted his head and looked down at the goddess, still wrapped tightly in Keira's bonds.

"Is she alive?" he asked, stalling for time. His hand tightened on his staff, sending the light into violent swirls yet again.

"Unfortunately," Ty muttered darkly.

"I have to say, I am impressed. I never thought the four of you stood a chance against her." Hades frowned down at them. "How did you do it, anyway?"

"Determination," Leo said. He pulled Hecate forward and flipped her around one-handed until she was upright, hanging limply from her bonds. He thrust her toward Hades. "Here. Take the witch-bitch and restore my soul. I'm ready to go home."

Hades eyed the goddess Leo presented before glancing at the staff in his hand, the soul inside it now swirling ever more excitedly. He ran his tongue over his teeth and indecision lit his dark eyes.

"You have a very unique soul. It has been eye-opening to be its caretaker these past weeks," he hedged. He really didn't want to give up Leo's soul. It might be worth reneging on his bargain with this human. He was a god, after all. What could this man do to stop him? Nothing.

His eyes snapped back to the group in front of him as the little one—Keira—marched around Leo, her eyes ablaze. Fury rolled off of her in waves. He resisted the urge to smile. She was cute. Like a mother hen, pissed at the fox for messing with her flock.

"You promised, you bastard. Either give Leo back his soul or I swear on all that's holy, I will let granny dearest go and I will help her bring you down." She smiled smugly. "Don't forget, we still have the belt."

Hades jaw clenched and his eyes flashed. Cute or not, she needed to watch her tone. "Don't threaten me, human."

Keira propped her hands on her hips. "I'm merely stating facts." She glared up at the god. "Now give Leo back his soul."

Hades laughed. The sound echoed off the marble floors and stone walls. Humans never failed to surprise him with their pluck. They let their emotions rule, which often led them to taking on more than they were capable of.

"You're cute. But belt or not, I am infinitely more powerful than your great-grandmother. You may win, but it will be at tremendous cost. Are you prepared to pay that cost?"

He couldn't hold back the grin as Keira's face morphed into one of rage. Leo grabbed her and pulled her back before she could claw his eyes out, as she so clearly wanted to do.

"Enough playing around, Hades. You and I both know you're going to give me back my soul, so just do it."

Hades cocked an eyebrow. "Really?" He studied the man in front of him. This one differed from his lady friend. He most definitely thought things through. Hades had learned that and much more about the facets of Leo Devereaux these last weeks. This man was not only thoughtful, but methodical and had a strong moral compass. He was also extremely powerful. More so than he knew. Hades had Athena and Artemis to thank for that, unfortunately.

Leo nodded. "Other gods are watching you. No matter how much you try to make yourself look like a loner down here in your dark kingdom, you still have contact with those on Olympus. You count on those contacts to get you what you want, to form alliances. If you go back on your word to me, how are they ever going to trust you again?"

Hades scoffed. "They will not care if I double-cross a mortal. You are beneath us all."

"Even a mortal who is your equal? One who could potentially kill you and take over your kingdom? I have all the powers of a god, Hades. I just have to be more careful about how I fight so I don't die. I would think a deal with me, someone who is a threat to any god, would hold some weight with your brethren above."

Hades frowned. Maybe Leo was aware of how powerful he was.

He straightened as the man stepped forward until they were toe-to-toe.

"I don't want your kingdom, Hades. I just want to go home and live my life. Do you really *need* my soul? Will having it as part of your collection really be worth the fight? The potential that you will lose?"

Hades weighed the man's words. He knew Leo was right, but he wasn't too keen about being called on his bullshit, especially by a human. He had smited lesser men for the same offense.

He searched the man's eyes, which stared at him unwaveringly. Determination, resignation, and a strength that surpassed any Hades had ever seen in any other human looked back at him. What was shockingly absent was fear. This man did not fear death.

It suddenly dawned on him that Leo knew he was destined for heaven, but could only achieve it if he had his soul. He essentially had nothing to lose by taking Hades on in a fight and would react accordingly. If Hades continued down this path and insisted on keeping Leo's soul, he would have quite the battle on his hands. One he may not walk away from.

A shiver of unease skated up Hades's spine. Apparently, he was the one who underestimated the power Leo held.

Shoving aside his anger at being called out by this man-god as well as his desire to keep the soul swirling angrily in his staff, he finally shook his head and took a step back. "You have more grit and honor than many gods, Leo Devereaux. Athena and Artemis knew what they were doing when they chose you for this fight. I will not renege on our bargain." He pulled the unconscious Hecate to his side before tipping his staff forward and touching it to Leo's chest.

The golden light flowed eagerly from the staff into Leo's body. Hades watched elation cross his face as he embraced his soul. It was nice to see someone appreciate what a precious gift the soul was.

When all the light had flowed back into his body, Leo opened his eyes and smiled.

Hades nodded once at him. "You are whole now, Leo. I wish you and your friends all the best. Thank you for all you've done."

A tinge of anger marred Leo's smile, but he wisely held his tongue. Grateful or not, Hades would not hesitate to defend his kingdom if pushed. Especially by a human, even if he was, technically, an equal.

Keira let out a little growl and lifted a hand, ready to give Hades a piece of her mind. He lifted an eyebrow at her just as Leo slapped his hand over her mouth and pulled her back into his chest before she could utter a word. She twisted her head to glare up at him.

He bent low to whisper in her ear. "Let it go. I got my soul. Let's just go home."

Her eyebrows dipped in a fierce frown before her face relaxed and she nodded. He let her go and took her hand.

Hades looked down at the tiny woman. She would be a good companion for Leo. Strong and independent, but wise, like the man at her side.

Ty and Penny stepped up to stand beside Leo and Keira.

"Hades, I'd say it's been fun, but it hasn't, really. You want to tell us how the hell we get out of here?" Ty practically growled.

Hades barked out a laugh. This one was cut from the same cloth as his friend. "I wish humans could know the kind of fearless defenders they have in you four." He motioned them forward. "Form a circle and hold hands. I will send you home."

Without a word, the four of them did as he said.

"I thank you again for all you've done. I'm sure the other gods thank you as well. You have saved us all." Hades's mind flashed to the note that had come to his attention shortly before their arrival. His eyes landed on the taller man who looked so much like the face Hades saw in the mirror every day. "And Ty?"

Ty looked up with a curious frown.

"I am truly sorry about your father. If it's any consolation, he will spend eternity as a very happy soul with your mother and sister."

Ty's jaw clenched and tears shimmered in his eyes. He offered Hades a small nod. "It is. Thank you."

Hades tipped his chin, then took a step back. "Safe travels, friends." He struck his staff to the ground. Wind swirled as the portal opened. He stepped back and watched as the four humans, who both aggravated and impressed him, were swept away.

When the wind calmed and the portal closed, Hades stepped over to the unconscious goddess who had collapsed to the floor with the absence of Keira's illusion, which kept her upright.

With one hand, he bent down and grabbed a handful of Hecate's dress at the waist and lifted her. Her body bowed, her hands and feet trailing on the ground as he carried her.

An evil smile covered his face as he headed for the entrance to his dungeon.

Time to have some fun.

CHAPTER 2

Hecate came awake with a start. Hades saw the moment she realized where she was. Her shackles clanked as she brought her hands up to touch the spot on her head where his human compatriots repeatedly knocked her out on their journey back to his palace. She froze, staring at the iron encircling her wrists. Her eyes glowed silver momentarily as she tried to access her powers. When they wouldn't work, she shrieked in rage and rattled the chains holding her to the cell.

He stepped out of the shadows.

"Hello, Hecate."

Her head snapped around to look at him, hatred pouring off of her in waves. He could already tell she was going to be hard to break. His smile deepened. Good. More fun for him. She deserved it after the hell she had wrought.

He unlocked her cell and stepped inside. She stood and faced him, still glaring. He admired her spunk. Most beings who found themselves locked in his dungeon pissed themselves before he even uttered a word.

"You won't win," she spat.

He held his arms out and looked around at the stone walls and iron bars that surrounded them. "Newsflash, sweet cheeks. I already did. Face it. You got beat by a bunch of demigod grandchildren. Now, you're mine."

She laughed.

"You keep telling yourself that, *Your Majesty*." She walked forward until the chain pulled taught. Only a foot away, she tilted her head back to look up at him, a smug smile on her face. "I'll find a way out of here. And when I do, you best watch your back."

He arched a brow and looked down at her. "No one has ever escaped my dungeon. You will not be the first."

She tossed a saccharine smile up at him. "Mmm-hmm. Sure. I'm not debating this with you. It's just a fact."

Hades muttered under his breath about bitchy women and rolled his eyes. "It's also a fact that I didn't bring you down here to talk, witch." His eyes began to glow silver and that evil smile crossed his face again.

Hecate's own eyes widened slightly at the change in his demeanor.

He thrust forward the hand holding his staff. An invisible wave of energy sent her flying against the cell wall. She hit with a thud and crumpled to the cell floor. He advanced and lifted her off the ground by her throat, pinning her against the wall before she could shake off the first blow. He touched his staff to her chest. The fabric of her dress burned away and her skin sizzled. A small wisp of smoke rose from her body, mingling with her scream of pain.

He pushed harder, sending the staff through her skin and into the muscle layer, then on down into the bone. Finally, he stopped just before it reached her heart. She writhed in his grip now, her features twisted in agony.

Not letting the pain recede, he touched the staff to her arm. More smoke rose. He continued his ministrations until burns and holes peppered her flesh and she was nothing more than a limp and nearly lifeless, sad sack of a being dangling from his hand.

Satisfied for now, he let go. She fell to the ground once again in a heap.

Eyes open to slits, she looked up at him, a measure of relief in her eyes.

"Oh, we're far from done."

She didn't have time to do more than furrow her brow questioningly before he snapped his fingers, sending her to one of the many torture chambers in the fiery pits of Tartarus. As much as he would love to spend eternity torturing her, he had other duties to attend to. Let the Hecatonchires use their hundred hands to rip her to pieces each day before magic put her back together for another round.

He strode from her cell, slamming the door behind him. The echo of metal clanging followed him as he walked down the dank corridors. Prisoners yelled out in pain and fear as his demons tortured them for their misdeeds. It was too bad Hecate was such a powerful goddess. He would have liked to have kept her here, where he could listen to her screams. She required a stronger hand, however. He would have to make a visit to Tartarus soon. To see how quickly his demons wiped that smug smile off her face.

A touch of unease ran along his nerve endings. She had been very sure of herself. So certain that it wasn't over. Her bravado had been something to see. But that's all it was.

Right?

He scoffed and ran up the stairs leading back to the main levels of his palace. What was he doing even entertaining the thought that there was more to come? She was in his dungeon and would never leave. Eventually, he would snuff out her existence after she paid for her mutinous behavior. There was no more threat to his kingdom or to the order in the realms. She was bluffing, trying to save face.

But her self-assured posture and the absolute lack of fear in her eyes kept that hum of unease from fully retreating. She might just have wanted him to think there was more at play, but he wasn't stupid. Regardless of whether or not he believed her, he would keep his ears open for more of her machinations.

He gave the door at the top of the stairs a shove. It banged off the wall behind it, the sound reverberating down the stone hallway. Several servants jumped and turned to see him bearing down on them. They scurried out of the way as his long legs carried him through the castle on his way to his room.

He needed a drink.

CHAPTER 3

Hades stared down at the courtyard from the window in the main floor living room. His wife walked up the path, an army of servants in tow, carrying her luggage. Her dress fluttered around her ankles, and she laughed at something her handmaiden said.

A feeling of peace descended upon him at the sight. He knew all the stories about him said he kidnapped Persephone from her mother because of her beauty. While that was what drew him to her in the first place, it was not what led him to coerce her to the underworld. She came of her own free will when he told her she gave him a feeling of serenity whenever she was around. That she balanced out the darkness around him and in his soul. It was only the stipulation that she could never leave that led to the animosity between them. Her mother meant the world to her, which is why they had come to the agreement she would spend half the year here and half the year with Demeter. Hades was always glad when summer ended.

He watched her a moment longer, happy to just look at her. She walked with a confidence born of her status. Her long legs ate up the ground. His servants, smaller in stature, scurried to keep up, their black limbs moving twice as fast.

In a blink, he was in the foyer. The doors opened, and she rose the last few steps and crossed the threshold.

He smiled broadly, happy to have her home again.

She strode toward him, a saucy smile on her face. "Miss me?"

He grabbed her and hauled her in tight against his body, his face close to hers. "You know I did." He crushed his mouth to hers, oblivious to the servants walking around them to take Persephone's belongings upstairs.

Her arms circled his shoulders, and she wrapped her legs around his waist. They might fight over a lot of things, usually pertaining to her inability to leave the underworld whenever she wanted and his hatred of her mother, but they had never lacked this spark. He had spent eternity with this woman and would never tire of the feel of her in his arms.

He broke their kiss and rested his forehead against hers. "How's your mom?"

Persephone threw back her head and laughed. She unwrapped her legs, but let her body skim his as she found her footing. He bit the inside of his cheek as she rubbed against the throbbing erection she had elicited.

She arched a brow at him and grinned knowingly.

He growled. "Minx."

She laughed again and spun away, her dark hair swirling behind her like a curtain as she headed for the kitchen.

He followed like a whipped puppy.

The high heels of her shoes echoed off the hallway walls as they walked. She glanced over at him and offered a cheeky smile. "Mom was ready to come down here and send you to your own dungeon. That descendant of Hecate? Keira? She came to our office to get my help in locating Hecate. I was getting ready to draw a map of her fortress when

Mom walked in, thinking it was some kind of agricultural meeting, and threw a monkey wrench into the works. She hated the thought of helping you—I did too, for that matter—but I'm a little easier to convince you're not a total bastard. Anyway, Mom was adamant it was all a ruse. That little spitfire must have been feeling the pressure of the deadline you imposed because she whipped out these vines that just—grew!—straight from the floor and bound Mom to her chair. Every time she tried to get a hand free, Keira just brought up more vines and kept her there. It was impressive."

They entered the kitchen and Persephone went straight to the fridge, pulling out a carton of strawberries and some milk. Hades leaned against the counter and watched her make herself a snack. Travel to and from the underworld always zapped some of her energy and made her hungry.

"After they left, she was ready to not only come down here and give you a beat down, but also go to Dad and tell him what was going on."

Hades's eyes widened.

Persephone nodded. "I know. That would have been bad. I managed to talk her out of both, but she said to tell you that you're an asshole and if it wasn't for the fact it would have upset the balance, she would have offered her services to Hecate."

He rolled his eyes. "Of course she would have. It's been millennia. When is she going to forgive me for falling in love with you?"

She cored the strawberry in her hands and plopped it into the blender. "Never. Just like I'm always going to resent the fact that I can't have both the freedom to move between worlds and you."

Hades swallowed down that bitter pill. He hated that the rules of the underworld prevented him from giving her what she so desperately desired. It killed him that, while he knew she loved him, she also hated him for keeping her from her family. That she was forced to live amongst the death—the sadness—that permeated this place because he had tricked her into staying, simply because he couldn't live without her.

She poured some milk in the blender, then spun around, taking a carton of vanilla ice cream from the freezer.

"Hermes told me the humans succeeded." She added a generous scoop of ice cream to the blender. "I feel bad for Hecate. She was my friend. But she had it coming. I can't believe she tried to take over—everything!"

Hades nodded, his mouth twisting as that familiar unease fluttered to life again. Nothing untoward had happened in the last few months since her capture, but he still couldn't shake the feeling that Hecate had something up her sleeve.

Persephone slapped the lid on the blender and turned it on, quickly whizzing together its contents. Pouring the mixture into a glass, she stuck a smoothie straw in it and took a slurp, moaning in delight.

"I love milkshakes," she murmured, looking at him seductively through her lashes as she sucked on the straw again.

Hades bit back a strangled groan. The erection he just got under control surged to life once more.

She laughed and set the milkshake on the counter, coming around to step into the circle of his arms.

He bent his head to kiss her, but she put a hand between them, covering his lips.

"Um. Persephone?"

"Why aren't you happy that Hecate's been stopped?"

He let her go and stepped away, cursing. Talk about a mood killer. Running a hand through his hair, he looked back at her.

"I am happy."

"Mmm-hmm. Sure. I've lived with you way too long to fall for that. Tell me what's going through that mind of yours."

Hades sighed and rested against the counter, hands pressed to the surface next to his hips. He looked down at the floor and huffed out a breath before looking back at his wife. "I think she has more planned."

Persephone frowned, her expression more serious now. "Like what?"

He shrugged and crossed his arms. "That's the thing. I don't know. It's just a feeling. When I first confronted her, she laughed and basically told me that while I won the battle, the war wasn't over."

"She was just bluffing. She's never liked to lose."

He tipped his head. "It was more than that. There was no fear in her eyes. Nothing that said she felt defeated."

Persephone walked closer and rested a hand over his folded arms. "She *did* fool us all for a very long time. Perhaps she is just that good of an actress."

He bit his lip, still not convinced. "Maybe."

"Well, did you find anything to indicate she might be telling the truth? I know you've put out feelers."

He shook his head. "There's nothing."

She leaned into him and ran her hands into his wavy hair. Hades felt some of the tension ebb as her long fingers caressed his scalp.

"I wouldn't worry about it, then. She's probably just bluffing."

He leaned down, his mouth inches from hers. "Probably."

"I wouldn't waste another thought on the bitch. Let her rot in Tartarus for the next few millennia."

"Okay." He narrowed the gap between their lips until only a breath separated them.

"You have more pressing things to take care of right now." She tilted her hips into his and he growled.

He saw her pupils dilate and her nostrils flare as he latched on to her mouth and pulled her into his body. Heat immediately shot to life between them and he spun, pinning her against the counter.

She moaned into his mouth, the sound going straight to his groin. He throbbed against his zipper, aching to feel her warm body surrounding him.

He trailed his fingers down her hip and bunched up the material of her dress until he reached the smooth skin of her thigh beneath.

She pulled back from his kiss on a gasp. "I can't wait."

A groan rumbled through his chest. "Me either." He ripped down the bodice of her dress, exposing her breasts. Taking one nipple in his mouth, he lifted her onto the counter and spread her legs, stepping between them. She held his head to her chest, urging him on with her moans.

He rucked up her dress to find she wasn't wearing any panties. A strangled groan got stuck in his throat. "You know I love it when you come home with no underwear on."

She smiled coyly. Her hand slipped between them to undo his belt. The hiss of his zipper echoed the hiss that slid between his teeth at the feel of her hand against his aching erection.

He latched onto the soft skin at her neck as she tugged him free of his clothes.

Hands on her butt, he pulled her to the very edge of the counter and quickly sheathed himself in her wet heat. Both of them moaned as their bodies reconnected after six months apart. He didn't give her a chance to recover from the invasion. Neither of them was going to last long. With sure, powerful thrusts, he soon brought them to the edge of paradise. A sharp bite to the tip of her breast sent her spiraling over the edge. The clench of her body around his sent him over his own precipice.

Hades sagged against her as his body melted from the pleasure. He had missed this. Missed *her*.

Soft hands stroked his back, and she nuzzled his neck, leaving a trail of kisses from his jaw to his collarbone.

"Welcome home," he whispered into her hair.

She laughed low in her throat. "Indeed."

Legs solidifying slightly, he straightened. Locking his hands under her thighs, he lifted her off the counter. "How about we continue this party upstairs?"

She bit his neck. "Yes, please."

His knees threatened to buckle, and it was only the thought of all the things he was going to do to her once in their bed that kept him from falling into a puddle on the floor.

In a blink, he was in their bedroom and throwing her onto the massive four-post bed that dominated the space, all thoughts of Hecate thoroughly forgotten.

CHAPTER 4

This couldn't be right.

Hades shuffled through the papers once more, looking at the totals. Something was wrong. The numbers were way off. He scanned through the reports again.

What the hell? The last quarterly report—around the time of Hecate's capture—was normal. But this last one—he had never seen a drop like this.

He fumbled for the phone on his desk and hit the speed dial number for Thanatos, absently marveling at how much he loved modern technology. It made things much simpler for them as well as the humans.

"'Sup?"

Hades frowned at the god's casual greeting. Would it kill the guy to say hello like a normal person?

"Has something happened on Earth I'm not aware of? The number of souls crossing through my gates has dropped dramatically in the last week."

"No, it's been business as usual up here. Hang on. I'll send you my spreadsheets for this quarter."

Hades's phone dinged, indicating a message. He pulled the device away from his ear to open it. Quickly scrolling through it, his unease grew. Thanatos's numbers looked normal. And in no way came close to matching his.

He put the phone back to his ear. "Okay. Thanks. Keep an ear out, would you? Something strange is going on."

"Will do, boss."

Hades hung up and tossed the phone down. Worry furrowed his brow as he stared down at the reports once more. Maybe Melinoe knew something. As the goddess of spirits, his daughter was responsible for helping the souls figure out where they were going. Some of them elected to stay behind and roam the Earth as ghosts, but most chose to cross the Acheron and enter his kingdom.

He picked up his phone again, dialing her number. It rang several times before her voicemail kicked in. Frowning, he hung up without leaving a message. She always answered for him.

Gathering the reports, he rose from his desk and stuffed them into his back pocket. He would go pay her a visit. Hopefully, she could make sense of what was happening.

He blinked out of the castle and was soon in the woods surrounding Melinoe's cottage. He had offered his daughter a room in the palace, but she refused. Said she wanted something quiet and secluded.

Water babbled in the nearby stream and birds chirped as he walked up the path to her house.

As he drew closer, he noticed the door was ajar.

Alarmed, he hurried forward. Nudging it open, he stepped inside. What greeted him was nothing short of complete chaos. Furniture was overturned, pictures broken. The curtains lay pooled on the floor, ripped from the rods.

His boots crunched on broken glass as he moved into the room.

"Melinoe?"

Silence greeted him.

He moved from room to room, searching for her, but all he found was more of the same destruction.

He stepped out the back door and scanned the forest. Nothing looked out of place.

"Melinoe!" His voice echoed through the trees. Birds scattered, and the wilderness went silent.

Genuine fear for his daughter had him spinning around and hurrying back to the castle. In an instant, he was pushing through the doors.

"Persephone!"

The walls rattled as his voice boomed through the castle.

Immediately, she was in front of him.

"Geez, Hades. Are you trying to bring the house down?"

"Have you talked to Melinoe lately?" he asked, ignoring her quip.

She shook her head, frowning. "No. Not in a couple of weeks. Why?"

"She's missing?"

Her eyes widened. "Missing? What? How do you know?"

He pulled the reports on the recently deceased from his back pocket and handed them to her. "The numbers coming through the gates are off. I called Thanatos and asked if he had noticed a decline in deaths, but he said no, so I called Melinoe. She didn't answer her phone, so I went to her house." A lump formed in his throat and he had to swallow hard to continue speaking. "When I got there, the door was open, and the house had been ransacked. It looked like she put up a fight. I called for her, but I didn't get an answer."

The pages in Persephone's hands shook as her hands trembled. "What do we do?"

"I'm going to call Ichnaea. See if she can track her."

"She'll want something for helping you."

"I know. I'm willing to pay that price if it means we find her." He would do anything—*anything*—to find his daughter. Taking out his phone, he scrolled through his contacts until he found Ichnaea's.

It rang several times before the goddess's no-nonsense voice came over the line.

"Hades. This is a surprise."

"Hello, Ichnaea. I'm going to cut straight to the chase. Melinoe is missing, and I need your help."

"Missing? You're sure."

He rolled his eyes. "Yes, I'm sure," he barked. He took a deep breath to rein in his temper. Berating the woman would not get him what he wanted. "I'm sure. Her house has been ransacked, and she's not answering when I call her. She always answers when her mother and I call."

"Meet me at the outdoor market in Larissa. I'll be by the baklava stand." She hung up.

"What did she say?" Persephone demanded.

"She wants me to meet her on Earth."

"I'm coming with you."

"Honey, you can't."

She shot him a withering frown. "You can make an exception to the terms of my imprisonment if I'm with you."

Hades sighed. "For the millionth time, you're not a prisoner. You're my wife. That means you're bound to my kingdom."

"I'm also bound to you. I will still technically be with the kingdom if I'm with you. We've done this before. Why can't we do it again?"

She wasn't wrong, but he hated taking her to Earth when she was in his kingdom. It made Zeus itchy. He was a stickler for rules and hated it when Hades found a way around them. And he didn't need his brother asking questions.

But it was very hard to say no to his wife's pleading brown eyes.

"Fine." He'd just deal with Zeus if his big brother stuck his nose where it didn't belong.

"Let's go." He took her hand and after a quick detour to get his staff from his office, sent them spiraling to an uninhabited area near the city of Larissa in the Thessaly region of Greece.

In a blink, they were in the city and moving toward the downtown market.

"Where are we supposed to meet her?"

"At the baklava stand in the market."

"If my stomach wasn't in knots, that would actually sound good."

He couldn't help the smile that tipped one corner of his mouth. It was a good thing his wife was a god and could eat whatever she wanted. He hated the thought of how moody she would be if she had to curb her snacking obsession.

As unobtrusively as he could, he wove them through the throng of humans out shopping. Many of them sensed the danger vibes his very presence projected and gave them a wide berth. A few, either ignoring the threat or oblivious to it, tried to talk to them. Hades ignored them all and pushed through the crowd.

"There she is," Persephone whispered, nodding toward the khaki-clad figure leaning against a building, shoving baklava into her mouth.

She spotted them and quickly gulped down the last of her treat. Sunglasses covered her face and a ball cap sat over her short, dark hair, shielding her face from the sun.

"Ichnaea," Hades greeted her.

"Hades. It's been a long time. And Persephone. How did you escape the underworld? It's winter."

"Technically, I'm still with it." She pointed at her husband.

"Will you help us?" Hades asked, skipping the small talk.

Ichnaea smiled. "Well, that depends. What are you going to give me for it?"

"What do you want?" Hades countered.

Ichnaea pulled her glasses down the bridge of her nose to stare at him in astonishment over the rim. "You're kidding, right? You're giving me carte blanche?"

"Within reason, yes." It chafed, but this was Melinoe.

She shoved her glasses back up and grinned. "Well, isn't this my lucky day? I want a pack of your hellhounds loyal to me."

Hades clenched his jaw as he stared at the smiling goddess. "I can't unleash those on the earthly realm. You know that."

She waved a hand. "Meh. I'll keep them on Olympus. Zeus will hate it." She cackled in delight at the thought.

He just stared down at her skeptically.

She huffed and crossed her arms. She tipped her head and looked at him over the top of her sunglasses. "You have my word, okay? If I take them anywhere near or on the earthly realm, you can have them all back. Deal?"

Hades looked at his wife, who nodded imperceptibly. He sighed and nodded, extending a hand. "Deal."

Ichnaea shook it enthusiastically. "Awesome. Okay. I need to see something of Melinoe's to track her. Being in her home would be better. I'll get a clearer trail."

Hades gave a short nod. "Come with us. We'll take you there." He whirled on his heel, not bothering to see if she followed. If she wanted those hounds as badly as he thought she did, she would be right behind them.

Faster than before, he pushed back through the crowd. His urgency made the humans even more wary of him, and no one bothered them as they walked through the market. As soon as they were clear of prying eyes, he moved at a more supernatural speed, quickly bringing them to the clearing where he and Persephone had arrived.

Striking his staff to the ground, he opened the portal and sent them all to Melinoe's house. When the debris settled, they were staring at his daughter's front door once again.

Persephone took his hand and held it tight. He squeezed it reassuringly and strode toward the door, pushing it open again.

Even though he knew what to expect, it still hit him like a punch to the gut to see the destruction throughout the house.

Ichnaea whistled low and long. "Somebody sure did a number on this place."

"Do your thing, Ichnaea. Find my daughter."

For once, she didn't have a quick comeback. Instead, she just nodded.

He stood off to the side and watched as Ichnaea accessed her abilities. The goddess's eyes glowed gold as she concentrated.

After a moment, she turned toward the back door. "This way."

Clutching Persephone's hand tightly, they trailed Ichnaea as she followed a path only she could see. Moving rapidly, they were across his kingdom in just moments.

As they cleared the mountains bordering the Asphodel Fields, he realized they were nearing Hecate's domain in his kingdom. The forests outside her fortress loomed before them. That unease he felt months ago came roaring back to life, louder than ever.

Ichnaea led them into the trees.

"It's eerie in here," Persephone whispered. "It wasn't like this before."

Hades felt it, too. Nothing moved. Nothing made a sound. There wasn't even a breeze. It was like the world was frozen around them.

Suddenly, Ichnaea stopped. Her spine went rigid, and she froze.

"What?" Hades let go of Persephone's hand and stepped forward. "What did you find?"

She didn't have to answer him. It was readily apparent why she stopped as soon as he pulled up next to her.

There, next to a pile of fallen trees, lay his daughter, staring sightlessly up at the sky.

The breath left his body, and he dropped to his knees. Agony tore through his soul as he stared at Melinoe's lifeless body, sprawled haphazardly over the ground. His thoughts ground to a halt, and he barely noticed as Persephone flew past him to fall to the ground near their daughter's body. Her wail of pain echoed through the forest. He watched as she touched Melinoe's body, beautiful even in death.

Finally, the fog cleared and anger took its place. He rose, body ramrod straight. Whoever had done this was going to pay.

He turned to Ichnaea. "Stay with her." He motioned to where Persephone lay weeping now, holding Melinoe's limp hand.

Not waiting for her acquiescence, he spun on his heel and blinked back to his castle. He made his way down to the dungeon to the cell where he had first kept Hecate. Standing in the middle of it, he snapped his fingers.

Hecate appeared on the floor in a heap. Blood ran in rivulets down her body. Chunks of her flesh were missing where the Hecatonchires had ripped it away, and her left arm hung by the skin from her shoulder.

Through pain-filled eyes, she looked up at him. A smirk lifted one side of her mouth and some of the pain receded.

"Hey. Don't tell me you've decided to torture me yourself again."

He bent down and picked her up by her throat. She dangled from his grasp, clutching at his arm with her good hand. "What did you do?"

She tried to smile, but it came out as a grimace as she gasped for air. "What—what do you mean? I've—been—locked up."

He growled. His senses had opened, and he knew his eyes were swirling silver as he held the goddess's life in his hands.

He shook her like a rag doll. She choked and her eyes bulged.

"Tell me what you did!"

She scratched at his arms, mouth working like a fish. He loosened his hold so she could speak.

Sucking in a breath, she looked up at him, satisfaction gleaming in her weary eyes. "I told you it wasn't over."

"My daughter is dead. Tell me why I shouldn't snap your neck like a twig and end your miserable existence." His hand tightened, and she gurgled.

He let up again, and she coughed. "Because you'll never find her soul if you do."

"What?" A deadly calm entered his voice.

She grinned. "You want to find her soul? Bring her back to life? Well, you're going to have to give me something."

He resisted the urge to remove her head from her body. "You said you would never lose to a pack of humans, either, so I don't think I believe you. So, I think I'll send you back to the Hecatonchires and tell them to be extra brutal while I go look for Melinoe's soul myself."

He raised his free hand, ready to snap his fingers, when she stopped him.

"Wait. You have a much more pressing concern to take care of first."

He moved her closer until their noses practically touched. "What else did you do?"

She attempted to shrug. "You'll see."

With a frustrated roar, he snapped his fingers and sent her back to the Hecatonchires before he killed her.

Thrusting his hands into his hair, he pulled at the strands, his thoughts a jumble. He knew he should have paid more attention to the uneasy feeling she had given him. Now, his daughter had paid the price, and he had more problems to deal with.

He needed to know more about what she had done. He needed to visit the Oracle. It wouldn't be a straight answer, but it would at least give him *some* direction.

On fleet feet, he flew up the stairs, stopping only long enough to grab a stack of human money from the safe in his office. The Oracle, Pythia, had fully embraced modern human culture and loved to shop. She would gladly help him with anything if he paid her enough.

With the money clutched in his hand, he struck the ground once more with his staff and reopened the portal to Earth, thankful that night had descended for the humans. Pythia hid out in a secret cave that wasn't far from the ruins the humans flocked to at Delphi. He did not want to be seen and had no desire to wait until the peasants left.

Landing in front of the entrance to her cave, he didn't wait for the debris to settle before he strode inside.

"Pythia!"

Absently, he noted the changes she had made since he was last here. It had been quite a while since he had a reason to visit her. Modern art lined the smooth walls of the cave, and electric lights lit up the hall. Thick carpet cushioned his footfalls and silenced the echo of his voice.

She appeared in the doorway to a room ahead of him on the left.

"Hades? What are you doing here?"

"I need to speak to you. It's urgent."

She motioned him forward. "Come in. Please." She led him into a large living room. Like the hall, modern style greeted him from the art to the furniture. He couldn't help but wonder just how many times his older brother had visited Pythia in the last few centuries for her to have such lush furnishings.

"Sit down, please."

He shook his head. "No." He held out the bundle of cash. She took it from him, frowning.

"Hecate did something to my daughter from Tartarus. Her soul has been split from her body and is missing. When I confronted her about it, she told me that the war was not over. *You* told me that once those four humans captured her, it would be done. Why isn't it done? She mentioned something about there being a pressing matter I needed to see to—more pressing than finding Melinoe's soul—but she wouldn't tell me what it was. I need you to tell me what it was."

Pythia blinked at him silently for a moment. "Well. Okay, then. As far as the prophecy involving the four humans, that is done. She has been stopped and can no longer take over your kingdom or upset the balance of the realms *from that plan*. However, it sounds like she had a back-up plan. One that I did not foresee."

"You think?" He ran a hand through his hair and held the other out to the goddess in a placating manner. "I'm sorry, Pythia. I'm just very frustrated and very upset. I need some answers. Please."

She nodded, laying the money down on the table in front of the sofa. "Come with me and I will see what I can tell you."

She led him out of the room through a door at the back, taking them deeper into the cave. This passageway was much less modern, retaining much of its original stone structure. Only the lights shining brightly overhead spoke to the modern times in which they lived.

He followed as she made several twists and turns through the passageways until, finally, they ended up at her altar. Steam rose from the aqua blue pool of water behind the altar. He could feel the heat it put off as they neared it.

Without a word, Pythia unbuckled the belt at her waist and the fabric of her dress loosened. She let it fall open and shrugged it off of her shoulders to stand before him completely naked.

She motioned to the altar. "Stand here."

He moved to do as she said, while she walked into the water, submerging herself up to her neck. Once she reached the middle of the pool, she floated on her back, eyes closed.

He stood watching and waiting while she floated silently. The tips of her breasts rose above the water and her hair fanned out behind her.

Suddenly, she opened her eyes, the brown now a gleaming gold as she unleashed her abilities.

"I see death. A great war upon mankind." Her voice echoed through the chamber.

A bad feeling settled low in the pit of Hades's stomach. He had a good idea where she was going with this.

Her next words confirmed his hunch.

"Your human friends. And their friends. They are necessary to stop the apocalypse."

Hades crossed his arms and bowed his head, resting his forehead on his fingertips. "Great," he muttered. He had nothing against the quartet he sent after Hecate, but they would not be happy about having to help him once again.

Leo Devereaux's face popped into his head. That man—he left without a fight three months ago, but he wasn't so sure things would be the same this time around. Hades had no hold over him now. Nothing to convince him his help was required. If he tried to take Leo's soul again, it would not end in Hades's favor. Not now that Leo had the powers of a god. Hades was not prone to be wary of any human, but Leo gave him pause. He didn't back down from a just fight and he had the power to back it up. No, taking the man's soul or that of his loved ones was no longer an option. He would have to find another way to convince him and his friends to help.

"Can you see who is behind the plan, Pythia?"

She was silent a moment longer.

"Two gods. I can't see who. They are working with a human. In your friends' backyard."

The glow left her eyes, and she sat up. She blinked several times, then strode from the pool, water sluicing from her toned body.

Hades paid her naked frame little attention. His thoughts were already on how he was going to convince that quartet of humans he needed their help.

He held Pythia's dress out to her as she fully emerged from the water.

"Thank you, Pythia." He turned to leave, but her voice gave him pause.

"I wish you luck, Hades. This will not be easy. For you or for your human friends."

He looked over his shoulder at her. "Did you see anything about my daughter? About where her soul is?"

Pythia smiled sadly. "Only that she is lost and that it will take much searching to bring her home. Do not lose hope, for she is closer than you think."

What the hell did that mean?

He resisted the urge to roll his eyes. He hated the Oracle's cryptic talk. It wasn't her fault, though. She was bound by the laws that governed them all to only reveal the events that would not change the course of history. It gave him hope the humans would be successful since she gave him so much information about their opponent.

With a nod, he turned and left her. He needed more information before he went to the humans. There would be far less bitching from them if he could at least give them a name with which to start.

CHAPTER 5

He slammed through the door of his house, anger rolling off of him in waves. He'd had time to think as he traveled back from Earth. There was some great, sick cosmic joke being played on him, and he was tired of it. He wanted to track down the Fates and give them—especially Lachesis—a good lashing. He also wondered if Zeus had a hand in this. Sometimes, he got bored and decided to have a little fun. It would be just like him to get the Fates to mess with his lifeline.

A servant emerged from a room to his right as he walked down the hall to his office.

"Sire."

"Is my wife home?"

"Yes, sire. She is upstairs."

Hades whirled and headed for the main staircase. In a blink, he was standing outside their bedroom. He could hear Persephone crying within.

Tears welled in his own eyes, but he choked them back. The god of the dead did not cry.

Twisting the doorknob, he entered the room. His wife lay curled up on their bed, clutching a pillow. Tears streamed down her face and sobs wracked her body.

He went to her and laid down behind her, curving his body around hers to offer comfort.

"I'm going to find who did this, my love. They will pay."

She hiccupped as she swallowed her sobs and rolled to face him. The heartbreak on her face was his undoing. He felt a single tear trickle down his cheek.

Her hand came up to rest on his jaw. She wiped away the tear with her thumb.

"I know you will. I hope you make them suffer as no one ever has."

He kissed her forehead tenderly, then pulled her close. His heart ached both for the loss of his daughter and for how her death made Persephone feel. If he could take away her pain, he would.

"I want to talk to Hecate."

Hades pulled back to look down at his wife.

"No. That would not be a good idea."

She blinked up at him. "If you're worried about me seeing her torn up and bloodied, don't be. After what she's done, she's lucky it isn't me performing the torture."

"Why do you want to see her?"

"Because for centuries, she has been my friend. Maybe there's some shred of that left and she'll talk to me. I might be able to get us a name. Uncover who she sent to hurt you—us."

Hades weighed her request carefully. His dungeon was not a pleasant place. Persephone was no delicate flower, but she was—softer—than he was. Death and pain were his business. He lived it every day. Persephone only saw that from the periphery.

But she was right. She might be able to get something out of the reluctant goddess.

"Okay. But I'm going to be close by, just in case. That is not up for debate."

She nodded and sat up. "Let's go."

He looked up at her with a frown. "What? Now?"

She nodded again. "Yes. I want the bitch to fry." She poked him in the arm. "Let's go." She clambered off the bed and Hades rolled to stand beside her.

They made their way down to the dungeons to Hecate's cell. Hades cast a glance at his wife before snapping his fingers. Hecate appeared in front of them once more, the state of her body even worse than it had been earlier in the day. Her arm was completely missing now and her other hung limp. Her legs were at odd angles and her breathing came in quick, sharp pants. Blood covered her face. Pieces of her cheeks were flayed off and patches of her hair were missing.

"Back for more?" Hecate asked roughly. "Did you not get enough jollies by strangling me earlier?"

"I'm not here for that. Someone wanted to see you." He stepped aside to reveal Persephone standing in the doorway to the cell.

Hecate's eyes widened, and he saw a moment of tenderness cross her bloodied and swollen face before she quickly masked it.

"Did you come to take a piece of my hide as well?"

Persephone stepped forward and crouched down to Hecate's level. "No. I came to understand why you did it. I get that you hate Hades. Most of us do. But what I don't understand is why you would hurt me, too. I was your friend, Hecate."

Hecate scoffed, then coughed. Blood flew from her mouth and she moaned, panting heavily.

Swallowing hard, she offered Persephone a grim smile. "Because no matter what I felt for you, I hated him more. I hated *all* the gods more. I had a good life in the light before Artemis 'saved' me. She should have let me die as Dad's sacrifice. Instead, I got to spend eternity with the dead in this dank, dark, weird hellhole. I had a plan! Dad and all my other male relatives were off their rockers. It wouldn't have taken anything to turn them all against each other and kill them all off. I was going to be queen! I could have done so much. But the gods took all that away from me. So, I decided to take everything away from all of you."

She laughed softly. "This is far from over. You can torture me all you want, but it will still all come crashing down. Phobos and Deimos will create war on Earth and mankind will fall. Without them, you all are useless and will fade into *nothing*." She closed her eyes, a satisfied smile on her face. "We will all fade to nothing," she whispered.

Hades put a hand on Persephone's shoulder and pulled her up. Silently, they retreated from Hecate's cell. If she hadn't ordered the murder of his daughter, he would almost feel sorry for her. For the human girl she had been.

But she had murdered his child. He snapped his fingers and sent her back to her torturers.

"Did you hear what she said?" Persephone asked, her face hopeful. "Phobos and Deimos. She set Ares's sons upon mankind."

Hades's mouth twisted in a frown. He heard, all right. What he didn't understand was how. The twins didn't do anything without their father's approval. He wondered if Ares knew what they were up to.

"I heard. I'm going to send Ichnaea to Charleston and see if she can find them."

"Charleston?"

He nodded. "Pythia said the gods Hecate unleashed are operating in our human friends' backyard. The only humans I would even consider close to that category are the quartet who apprehended her. She also said the twins are working with a human to unleash this war. That should give Ichnaea some direction."

"She helped me bring Melinoe's body home, then said she would stay awhile to make sure I was okay. She was in the kitchen when I went upstairs to be alone. I think you owe her an extra-large pack of hellhounds. She's been wonderful."

He quirked an eyebrow. "Yeah, well, I think after I send her to Earth to look for Phobos and Deimos, I'm going to owe her more than that." He took her hand. "Come on. Let's go see if she's still around."

Ready to get this show on the road, they blinked to the kitchen. Ichnaea sat at the large center island munching on a sandwich and scrolling through her phone. She looked up as they entered.

"Hey. You're back. What'd you find out? I'm assuming you went to see Hecate."

He nodded. "And Pythia. We need your help again. Hecate convinced Phobos and Deimos to unleash a war upon mankind. They have the help of a human. I don't know who is or what his role is, though. I need you to find the twins and the human for me. We think they're in Charleston, South Carolina."

Ichnaea stuffed the last of her sandwich into her mouth and chewed thoughtfully.

"Our bargain was for me to find your daughter," she said once she swallowed. "I did that."

He nodded once. "You did. But I still need your help. If the twins succeed, we have bigger problems than bringing Melinoe's killer to justice. You won't get much use out of those hellhounds if we don't stop him."

She made a face of distaste and nodded. "Fine. But I want to visit the Asphodel Fields when this is done."

Hades frowned and stared hard at her, trying to understand why she would make such a request. Gods didn't visit human souls in the afterlife. They rarely had contact with them when they were living.

She crossed her arms and lifted an eyebrow as he continued to stare at her. Her face gave nothing away.

He scrubbed a hand over his face. "I suppose that is acceptable. But only you. You cannot bring or take anyone—living, dead, or in between—with you."

She held out a hand. "Deal."

He took it, praying he wasn't making a mistake in granting her wish.

Rising from her stool, she stuffed her phone into her pocket. "Okay, big man. Send me to Charleston."

He eyed the goddess for a moment, taking measure of her. Determination glinted in her dark eyes, her jaw set.

With a nod, he struck the floor with his staff. Wind swirled as the portal opened.

"Thank you, Ichnaea. I am most grateful."

She smiled cheekily. "Anytime."

The wind reached a fevered pitch before collapsing and taking Ichnaea with it.

"Now what?" Persephone asked as the air settled around them.

"Now, we wait until she calls me to bring her back. Hopefully, this doesn't take too long."

Almost before the words were out of his mouth, his phone rang.

He accepted the call. "That was fast."

"Not much to see," Ichnaea responded. "Bring me back." She hung up.

He stared down at his cell. No one had any phone etiquette anymore. Setting it on the counter, he struck the floor with his staff once again. In moments, Ichnaea stood before them.

"What did you find?" he demanded.

"Very little."

"Wait," Persephone said. "How were you able to even look for him? You needed to see something of Melinoe's to find her."

"On Earth, gods leave a trail for me to see, even if I don't have an item they recently touched. I got a tiny hit at a lab near the university. They were definitely there. I got inside and their trail was all over the office of a Dr. Brandon Henley. It went cold from there, though. Just disappeared."

Hades frowned. "How is that possible?"

She shrugged. "They can either open portals like you or something is obscuring their trail. My money's on the latter. Only you and your brothers can open portals outside your temples."

"That makes sense," Persephone said. "Hecate probably put a spell on them or gave them some kind of elixir to hide them."

Ichnaea nodded. "They probably have to renew it every so often. Or the trail leaks if they stay in one place for too long."

Hades ran his hands through his hair. "Okay. Thank you, Ichnaea. You've been a great help. Are you ready for your reward?"

"You're welcome. And, yes."

He brought up a hand, ready to snap her to the Asphodel Fields, but paused to look at her curiously. "Why do you want to go to the Fields, anyway?"

She drew in a breath and offered him a shaky smile. "Let's just say it involves an old friend and leave it at that."

His eyes narrowed slightly, but he did not press her for more information. Instead, he nodded. "Well, I wish you luck in finding who you seek. Call me when you are ready to return to Olympus." With that, he snapped his fingers, sending her to the Asphodel Fields in search of the human soul she sought.

He turned to Persephone. "I think it's time we pay our human friends a visit."

She gave him a coy smile. "You're going to play nice this time, right?"

He answered her smile with one of his own and struck the floor with his staff, opening a portal to Earth. "I make no promises."

***

Keep reading for a sneak peek of book 3 in the *Hecate's Rebellion* series, *The Dreamcatcher*.

PROLOGUE

L eo Devereaux came awake with a start. His eyes traveled over the bedroom in search of what pulled him from sleep. Wind rattled the window in its frame and buffeted the house.

What the hell?

He sat up, frowning. The forecast for the night was calm, clear weather. He shouldn't be hearing anything but the soft sound of Keira breathing as she slept.

The window rattled again, harder, and the roar grew.

A glance at his wife revealed she was still asleep.

Quietly, so as not to wake her, he got out of bed and crept to the window to look out. Looking through the glass, the stars glowed in the night sky, but the barren tree branches waved in the wind. Dust, grass, and leaves swirled in the yard, lifting up into the dark sky.

As the cloud of debris coalesced, a feeling of dread filled Leo's gut. He had seen this before.

Watching silently, he waited, hoping he was wrong about what was coming, but knowing he wasn't. The debris swirled in an ever-tightening column, lifting higher until it surpassed the tree tops. The wind reached a fevered pitch, then the mass of swirling debris collapsed to the ground in a violent rush, scattering the leaves across the yard. A man and woman emerged from the dust, their tall forms moving with an elegance and grace toward the house.

"Well, fuck."

Turning away from the window, he strode back to the bed and shook Keira awake.

She grumbled at him and swatted at his hand.

"*Chère*, wake up. We've got company."

Her eyes fluttered open. "What?"

He threw her robe at her. "Put that on and your slippers and meet me downstairs."

"Leo, what's going on?"

"Hades is here."

She jackknifed, the air around her crackling with her anger, and her eyes took on a slight silver glow. "Goddammit. What the hell does he want? I swear, if he tries to take your soul again, I'm going to smite him where he stands." She shoved off the covers and stood. Leo's eyes drifted to her belly and the tiny life growing there, reminding him they had a lot more at stake now.

One corner of his mouth quirked as he pulled on a pair of jeans and stuffed his feet into some shoes. His fierce kitten. "Considering I'm his equal now, he'll have a hell of a fight on his hands from me first. I'm going to wake Ty and Penny."

She nodded, hopping slightly as she wiggled her foot into her slipper while trying to thrust her arms into the sleeves of her robe.

Striding down the hall, Leo stopped in front of Ty and Penny's bedroom. He rapped on the door before turning the knob and throwing it open.

Ty jerked awake. Blue flames licked brightly in his eyes before he realized who had intruded into his bedroom.

"Leo. What the hell?"

Penny stirred beside him. "What's going on?"

"Hades just landed outside. He brought Persephone with him."

Ty's epithet matched Leo's. Tossing the covers aside, he climbed out of bed and pulled a pair of athletic shorts out of the dresser.

"What the hell does he want now?"

Leo shrugged. Ty's guess was as good as his.

A loud pounding sounded through the house as Hades banged on the front door.

"Guess we're going to find out. I'll meet you downstairs." Spinning on his heel, he caught Keira's hand in his as she burst out of their bedroom, and ran down the hall. Together, they hurried down the stairs. The Christmas lights wrapped around the railing lit their way.

Hades banged again.

"Humans! Open the door."

Leo rolled his eyes. Even after all they did for the bastard, he still spoke to them like they were dirt beneath his boots.

The sound of Ty's heavy footfalls on the stairs had Leo striding forward to open the front door.

What he saw on the other side had him biting back the scathing rebuke on the tip of his tongue. Hades's hair was disheveled and his clothes rumpled, while Persephone looked as though she had been crying.

"May we come in?" Hades asked, his voice tired.

Hesitating only a moment, Leo nodded and stepped back.

Penny flipped on the lights and led them all into the living room.

Ty motioned for the gods to sit.

Like someone pulled the stuffing out of her, Persephone sank onto the sofa. Hades perched on the edge next to her, wringing his hands.

Alarmed, Leo sat in the chair adjacent to them. Something was very wrong.

Keira, Penny, and Ty settled onto the other sofa, opposite Hades and Persephone.

Leo shared a look with Ty, who had the same concerned expression on his face.

"What's going on? Why are you banging on my door at three a.m.?" Ty demanded.

Hades glanced at his wife, who poked him in the arm and nodded, glancing at them.

Running a hand through his hair, the god sighed. Leaning an arm on his thigh, his mouth flattened distastefully before he spoke.

"We need your help."

"Why?" Leo asked. "I thought we were just a pack of humans."

Hades smiled ruefully. "You are. But you're a useful pack of humans."

Persephone punched him in the arm. "Not helping."

Holding his hands up in supplication, Hades huffed out a breath. "Okay. Sorry." He sucked in a deep breath and continued. "It seems Hecate had a longer reach than I originally thought. Before the four of you captured her and brought her to me, she launched another plan. A backup, of sorts."

Dread pooled in Leo's stomach. "What kind of plan?"

"She set Phobos and Deimos loose on Earth."

"Who now?" Ty asked.

"Phobos and Deimos. They're Ares's twin sons. Fear and dread. They induce panic wherever they go. Those riots in Turkey and Greece earlier this month? That was them."

"Okay. Why do you look so upset? You're not exactly in love with the human race."

He looked at Persephone and took her hand. "Lately, I noticed a decline in the number of souls coming through my gate. Figuring they were going somewhere, I went to see our daughter, Melinoe, the goddess of spirits, to ask if she noticed an uptick in the number of ghosts roaming Earth. When I reached her home, no one was there, and it looked like there had been a struggle. We searched for her, but—"

He took a shaky breath. Tears welled in Persephone's eyes.

"We found her in some sort of strange stasis in the forests outside Hecate's compound." Blinking furiously, he continued. "I confronted Hecate, and she admitted she put plans in place as a backup should she get caught. She wouldn't say what all she had done, but I managed to uncover that Phobos and Deimos, at her request, somehow split Melinoe's body from her soul. I've scoured the underworld for her soul, but can't find it. I fear if we don't reunite it with her body soon, she will die forever. Hecate wanted to hurt me and knew the only way to do that was through my family."

Leo closed his eyes briefly. He didn't want to feel for Hades, but he did. If something ever happened to the baby Keira carried, it would utterly devastate him. "I'm sorry, Hades. How is it possible that she could die, though? I mean, she's immortal, like you, right?"

"Any god can be killed under the right circumstances. From what we can figure, they frightened her so much it caused the split. But until we—" he broke off and cleared his throat. "Until we find her soul, we won't know for sure."

Persephone sucked in a breath and stood, pacing to the window.

Leo watched her for a moment before turning back to Hades. "Do you know what they're planning, then? Or was it just to hurt you?" Leo asked, switching gears.

"Hecate refused to tell me anything, so I sent out a scout to track them and find out what they were up to. I couldn't find their location, but I learned that they have enlisted the help of a mortal man,

Brandon Henley, a descendant of Hypnos. The man is a psychiatrist, specializing in hypnotic treatment for mental disorders."

Ty's curse was loud and long. "That's awesome. So, we have a doctor—who basically messes with people's minds—with supernatural abilities. And here I thought we were unique."

Hades pointed at Leo. "*He* is unique. The rest of you are just three of many others with divine blood running through your veins. You have just unlocked your abilities. Many people don't even know they have them. Or, what they do have is just a heightened version of something normal, like speed, or a genius IQ. There are very, very few of you who know what you actually are."

Leo frowned at that, but pushed it to the back of his mind to contemplate at a later date. "Okay. So, if Henley's working with Phobos and Deimos, I take it he's inducing panic in his patients?"

Hades's nod was short and succinct.

"I fail to see how this requires our attention. I mean, I get you want them caught so they can face punishment for what they did to your daughter, but are they really an imminent threat to mankind? Seriously, how many people can Henley hypnotize at once?"

"And why us again?" Penny asked. "We fulfilled the prophecy we were part of."

Hades shook his head. "Given the right platform, he could hypnotize quite a few people. And it wouldn't be normal hypnosis. He'll have a greater influence on people's minds. Theoretically, he could make anyone do whatever he wished. As for why I—need the four of you, you'll have to take that up with the Oracle. When this new development occurred, I went to her and asked if this was a legitimate threat. She said yes, and that I needed you again." He shrugged. "I don't argue with the Oracle. That's Zeus's thing. I've learned I never win. So, here I am. Asking for help." The last part came through gritted teeth.

Leo rubbed his temples. "That's just fucking fantastic. You realize Keira's pregnant, right? I'm not willing to put her in the line of fire. I didn't want to the last time, but with the life of our child on the line, you can forget it. And even from behind the scenes, I don't know how much help she'll be. The pregnancy is screwing with her abilities."

Hades's expression turned grim. "I'm afraid you may not have much of a choice. The twins will likely bring the fight to you. After what happened this past summer, they know you four are the only ones on Earth who can stop them."

Pushing to his feet, Leo paced to the window to stare out at the still night.

"You won't be alone, though, this time," Hades continued.

Leo glanced back. "What do you mean?"

"The Oracle mentioned the four of you and *some of your friends*. I don't know who they are, but I think one of them is Dr. Henley's associate, Dr. Clary Moncrief. You need to go get Dr. Moncrief and bring her here. She is in grave danger. She has figured out that Dr. Henley is up to no good. My scout saw her fleeing their research facility yesterday afternoon. She was apparently quite terrified."

Keira immediately stood. "I'll go get my scrying materials."

Leo held out a hand. "*Chère*, hang on a second." He hated the idea they didn't have a choice in this, but he wanted to make sure they were all on the same page before jumping into the fire.

He motioned the others toward the door and looked at Hades. "Give us a minute."

Leading the others out of the room, he headed for the foyer in hopes they could talk privately. They stopped at the base of the staircase.

"Are we seriously considering partnering with the devil again?" Ty asked, his voice low.

"I don't think we have a choice," Keira said. "If what he says is true, mankind is in trouble—big trouble—if we don't."

"Are you sure you can do what needs to be done?" Leo asked. "Your abilities haven't exactly been reliable lately."

Keira ran a hand over the slight swell of her stomach. Leo's heart clenched with a deep and fierce love, just like it did every time he thought of the life growing inside of her. Her pregnancy hadn't been planned, but it definitely wasn't unwelcome. He couldn't wait to meet their child.

"Even with the havoc this child has wreaked on my abilities, I still think I need to try. What kind of world will we be bringing this little one into if I don't? Will there even be a world to bring him into? The way Hades talked, we could be facing a global war."

Leo pursed his lips, not pleased with this turn of events. Putting his pregnant wife in the middle of a fight amongst the Greek gods was not something he was keen on. But she was right. If they didn't help Hades, their child would be born into chaos.

"All right, but you're staying out of the action. Something goes down, you are getting locked in the bunker." After what happened over the summer, Ty had a safe room installed in the house that was damn near physically impenetrable. Keira warded it to make it magically impenetrable. Leo was adding one to their house in Louisiana as well. He wasn't about to leave his family vulnerable. Not now that he knew what hidden evils there really were in the world.

Keira narrowed her eyes at him, not liking being told what to do. "If I'm not needed, I will gladly stay out of the way."

Leo arched a brow. "Even if you are, you're going to stay out of it. I'll rig up something in the bunker so you can still be involved, but from a safe distance."

She bit the inside of her cheek, but nodded.

He eyed her warily, not sure if she had acquiesced because she agreed with him or because she was trying to placate him. It never boded well for him when she capitulated so easily.

"So, are we doing this, then?" Ty asked, breaking into Leo's thoughts.

Keira nodded before Leo could open his mouth. "Yes. I don't want to give birth to this child, only to bring him up in a war zone."

Leo didn't either.

"So, who are these friends he's talking about? Colin is the only one who knows about what we really are," Ty said, mentioning his partner.

Leo shrugged. "I'd say that's certainly possible. He did help some with Hecate."

Ty nodded. "Let's go tell Hades, then I'll call Colin and have him come over."

"I'll go get my scrying stuff." Keira scampered up the stairs to her magic room.

Re-entering the living room, Leo, Ty, and Penny stood shoulder to shoulder and faced the powerful deities who had come asking for their help. Persephone still looked utterly miserable, while Hades just looked exhausted. Leo couldn't help but think how human they looked at that moment.

He quickly shut down that line of thinking. They were far from human, and it would do him well to remember that.

Taking a deep breath, he stared straight at Hades. "We'll help."

AFTERWORD

Thank you for reading *The King*! I hope you enjoyed it. Please consider leaving a rating or review. It would be greatly appreciated!